What's Missing?

written by
Nancy Louise Spinelle
illustrated by
Jenny Campbell

KAEDEN ❤ BOOKS™

Let's fix a snack.
I will set the table.

The plates are on the table, but something is missing.

Knives!

The knives are on the table,
but something is missing.

Bread!

The bread is on the table,
but something is missing.

Peanut butter!

The peanut butter is on
the table, but something
is missing.

Jelly!

The jelly is on the table,
but something is missing.

Glasses and milk!

The glasses and the milk
are on the table.

13

The plates, the knives, the
bread, the peanut butter,
the jelly, the glasses and
the milk are on the table.

What's missing?

You and I!